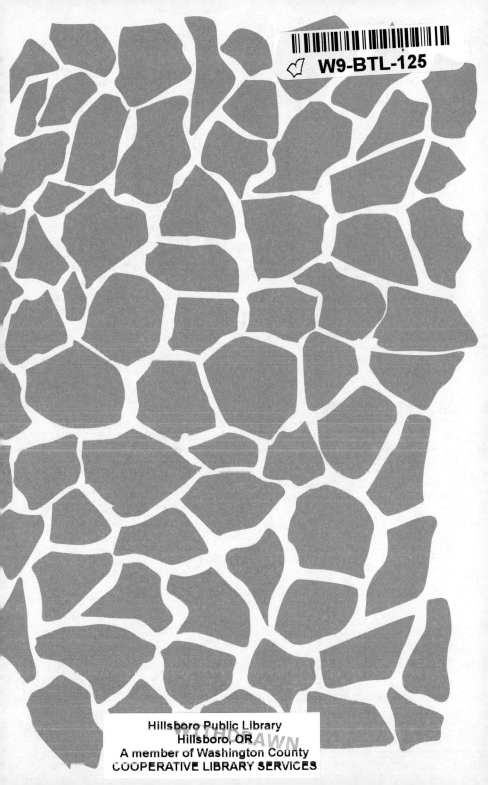

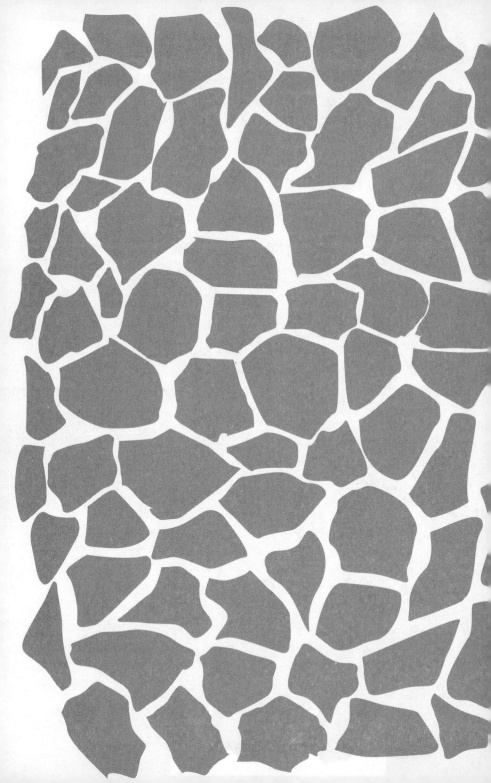

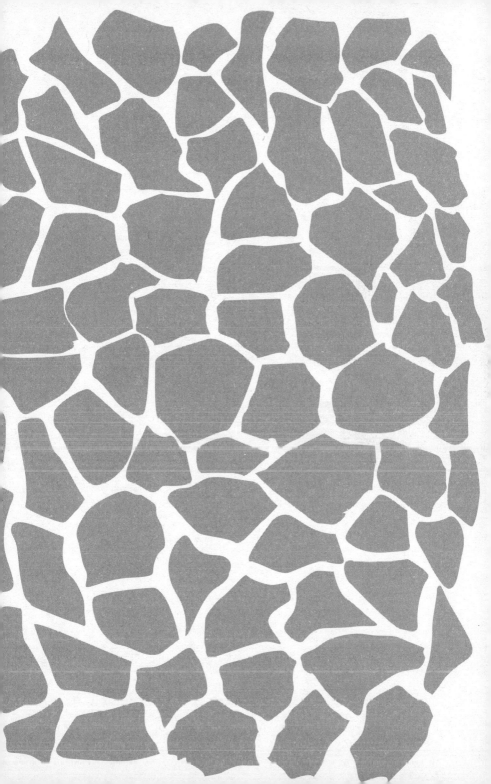

MYSTERIES ON ZOO LANE

#2

Animal at Large

#2
MYSTERIES ON ZOO LANE

Animal at Large

Patricia Reilly Giff

illustrated by
Abby Carter

HOLIDAY HOUSE • NEW YORK

HOLIDAY HOUSE is registered in the U.S. Patent and Trademark Office.
Printed and bound in January 2021 at Maple Press, York, PA, USA.
www.holidayhouse.com
First Edition
3 5 7 9 10 8 6 4 2
Library of Congress Cataloging-in-Publication Data
Names: Giff, Patricia Reilly, author. | Carter, Abby, illustrator.
Title: Animal at large / by Patricia Reilly Giff ; illustrated by Abby Carter.
Description: First edition. | New York : Holiday House, [2020] | Series:
Mysteries on Zoo Lane ; book #2 | Audience: Ages 7-10. | Audience:
Grades 2-3. | Summary: When Tori's cousin and best friend, Sumiko,
visits, the two girls investigate a mystery involving a missing zoo
animal and strange noises in the back yard.
Identifiers: LCCN 2019046314 | ISBN 9780823446674 (hardcover)
Subjects: CYAC: Zoos—Fiction. | Cousins—Fiction. | Friendship—Fiction.
Family life—Fiction. | Zoo animals—Fiction.
Mystery and detective stories.
Classification: LCC PZ7.G3626 Tt 2020 | DDC [Fic]—dc23
LC record available at https://lccn.loc.gov/2019046314
ISBN: 978-0-8234-4667-4 (hardcover)
ISBN: 978-0-8234-4908-8 (paperback)

33614082370080

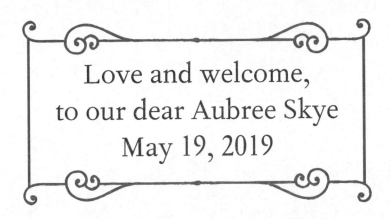

Love and welcome,
to our dear Aubree Skye
May 19, 2019

Animal at Large

CHAPTER 1

TORI was painting her nails. She had to be perfect. So did her room.

But what was on the floor?

Drops of Sparkle Red polish!

Never mind. She'd move the little rug next to her bed. It would cover the drops.

Her cousin Sumiko was coming from Japan.

She had come last year too. She'd drawn pictures of the zoo animals: bobcats, tigers, a pink flamingo.

Tori had tacked them up over her bed.

Now Tori's brother, Ken, stood at her door. "What a mess." He grinned. He didn't mind messes.

She dabbed polish on her pinkie. "What are you talking about?"

"Kimi's footprints are all over the floor."

Tori looked down at the floor. That cat! Tori would need a rug as big as New York to cover them.

Maybe that old rug in the basement. It had pictures of birds and their names. It was probably full of dust.

From her window she could see the zoo.

Kangaroos jumped around in Hopping Place.

A rhino wallowed in the mud. When the mud dried, it would cover its skin. Bugs would stay away!

Poor rhinos. Not that many were left in the world.

People had cut off their horns, or killed them to get their horns.

Now zoos were keeping them and their babies safe.

Tori spread polish on her thumbnail. She waved her fingers. Even her knuckles were Sparkle Red!

How did that happen?

She went out to the patio and poured seed into the feeder. Purple finches and catbirds were waiting.

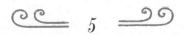

She sank down at the table, yawning. The sun was hot. She couldn't keep her eyes open.

She took off her glasses and put her head down on the cool table. She spread out her damp fingers.

Then, was she dreaming?

A leopard came out of the huge sticker bush.

It crouched next to her. It chewed on her nails.

A snake was wrapped around her thumb.

Tori's eyes flew open.

No leopard.

No snake.

She looked at her nails.

She couldn't believe it.

No red on her thumb.

None on her pinkie. The rest looked like polka dots!

Who had done that?

The door was four steps away.

She dived into the house.

CHAPTER 2

AT the airport, Tori saw Sumiko rushing toward her. They threw their arms around each other as Mom smiled.

Someone stepped on Tori's toes.

"Luke!" It was the new kid on Zoo Lane.

"Sorry. My grandfather is

coming from Florida." He dashed away.

"When we get home"—Sumiko stopped for a breath—"let's go right to the zoo. I'm dying to draw an ostrich."

"Good idea," Tori's mom said.

"I love the story of the ostrich and the giraffe," Tori said.

"A true story," Sumiko said. "They're best friends, like you and me."

They stopped at the house. Sumiko left her suitcase in Tori's room. "Is that a new rug?"

"Not exactly," Tori said. She and

Mom had dragged it up from the basement, sneezing from the dust.

She didn't want to think about footprints and rugs. "Let's go."

Outside, it was almost too hot to breathe. Still, they rushed down the path.

"Whew," Sumiko said.

They passed Nana-Next-Door. "Glad you're feeding the birds," Nana said. "Some of them are near extinction. Even some birds we see all the time. The black-throated sparrow. The grackle."

Nana knew all about birds. She knew about all kinds of animals.

Tori turned to wave. She slid on a pile of leaves, and went down hard.

Was this something to write about? No. But this summer, she had to write her life's story for Miss Raymond.

She didn't want to think about her life story either.

She had a just-plain life. What could she say?

Sumiko could write a great story. She'd say she flew thirteen hours from Japan to New York.

She could tell about Mount Fuji, the volcano near her city.

She spoke Japanese and English.

Tori knew only one Japanese word, the one for thank-you.

She lay on the ground another moment.

Her knee had a sore as big as an apple.

Sumiko reached out to pull her up.

Tori brushed herself off.

"Arigatou." There! She'd used her Japanese word for thank-you.

They circled around the path. They watched otters splash in Cool Pool.

Lucky otters.

Tori wished they had a pool in her yard. All they had was the hose. It sprinkled tiny drops of water.

Sumiko was ahead of her now.

"I'm coming," Tori called.

Wait. A green paper was tacked to a tree. Some of it had torn away. What was that all about?

CHAPTER 3

TORI reached for the paper. She waved it at Sumiko.

"We'll think about this later," Sumiko said. "First the ostriches?"

Yes, ostriches, the biggest birds in the world. With their long, skinny legs, they could run faster than tigers. But they couldn't fly.

"I'll show their eggs too," Sumiko said. She drew a huge circle in the air. "Largest in the world."

Ostrich eggs were sweet, Nana-Next-Door had told her. But for every egg someone ate, there was one less ostrich baby.

They passed Grizzly Bear Gulch and kept going to Bird World.

"Wait," Tori said. "What's that sign?"

NO OSTRICHES TODAY
SORRY

"Too bad," she told Sumiko.

Instead they watched some finches fly under the huge net.

All of a sudden a crow snapped up a bug.

Sumiko pulled out her pad. "I'll draw that crow."

Tori watched her sketch quick lines. "Neat," she said.

Back home, Tori tacked it up next to the ones from last year.

"Let's sit on the patio," Sumiko said.

Tori thought about her dream. She looked at her polka-dotted nails. "I guess so."

Outside, Tori looked at the giant sticker bush.

Everything was quiet.

She turned on the hose.

The sprinkler would feel cool on their bare feet.

Kimi, the cat, stared at them from the window.

Once she'd eaten a sparrow, feathers to tail. But no more. Now she was an indoor cat, eating cat food.

Tori put the torn green paper from the tree on the patio table.

"Missing!" Sumiko read aloud.

"From the zoo? I hope it isn't dangerous."

"Me too." Sumiko shook drops of water off her feet. "I have to text my mom."

She went inside.

Tori stayed a little longer.

And then she heard someone say "Tough!"

At least she thought she did.

She turned her head.

Was it was coming from the sticker bush?

Was someone calling her tough?

CHAPTER 4

INSIDE, Tori picked Kimi up. "I'm glad you weren't out there," she whispered to the cat. "Something strange happened."

Kimi gave her a quick cat kiss. She jumped out of Tori's arms and padded away.

"Love you," Tori called after her.

Maybe her brother, Ken, had been outside.

He was at the kitchen table now, stirring a pot of pink goo.

He was always trying things. They never worked.

Sumiko leaned over, watching.

Tori leaned over too. "Did you call me tough?" she asked Ken.

He looked surprised. "You're not one bit tough. You're even afraid of flies!"

She shook her head. "Only the gigantic ones."

Maybe the voice was just another dream, she thought.

Bang!

Pink goo shot everywhere.

"Volcano!" Ken yelled.

He began to wipe up the lava with his shirt.

Tori and Sumiko took dish-cloths. They worked at the wall.

When they finished, the wall was still pink. So were the dishcloths.

They threw them into the sink.

Ken looked disappointed. "Nothing comes out right," he said.

"You can't be perfect all the time," Sumiko told him.

Tori was glad to hear her say that. But only for a moment.

She was worried.

Who was missing?

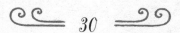

And who might be on the patio?

She thought of Mr. Stewart, the boss of the zoo.

He always said, "Use your brain."

Tori's brain told her . . .

Nothing.

But wait.

Maybe it was a kid.

Not Ken.

Not Alex. He was at the dentist. His teeth were a mess.

And Mitchell was at camp.

The only one left was Luke.

CHAPTER 5

TORI unlocked the door. She listened.

Sumiko was still talking to Ken.

No one was calling her tough.

Some scraps of paper blew toward her. They landed near the sticker bush.

She walked across the patio, but so slowly, she hardly moved. She took the papers and tucked them in her pocket.

Who was hiding behind the sticker bush? She had to find out.

She pulled a branch aside.

Ouch!

Her arm had a pink scratch.

Nothing there except stones and weeds!

Three more weeks until school

began. She wouldn't be out in the patio so much anymore.

But by then she needed a life story. If only she had something to say . . .

Something like:

I saved someone's life.

I won a million dollars. I gave it all to the zoo.

They needed ants for the anteaters.

The screen door flew open. It was Sumiko.

"I found more green papers." Tori said. She didn't have time to finish talking.

Sumiko was yelling. "I figured out what the papers say. It's bad news."

"What news?" Tori could feel her heart beating.

"Keep your eyes open at the zoo," Sumiko said. She grabbed the paper.

If only she could close them. But no!

They hurried into the zoo.

Sumiko slid to a stop at Ostrich Row. "Empty. I knew it."

"What?" Tori asked.

Sumiko held out the scrap of paper. "Look. O for ostrich! She

must be loose somewhere."

Now Tori did close her eyes. Was that who was hiding on her patio? What if the ostrich was hungry? Or angry? Would it come after them?

But Mom was calling. "Time for dinner."

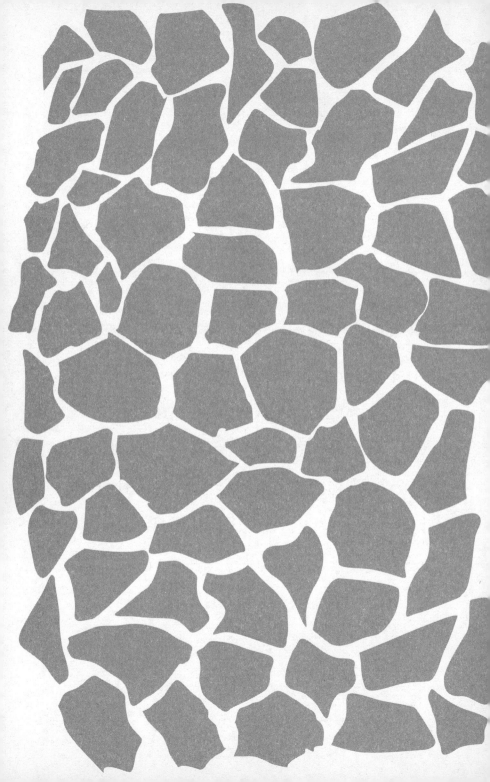

CHAPTER 6

THEY darted in the door.

"Salad and miso soup," Mom said.

Mom's salad was always crunchy; her miso soup was the best.

Under the table, Kimi lapped up kitty soup.

When they finished, Mom said,

"It's beautiful outside. You need fresh air."

"I guess . . ." Tori said.

She and Sumiko looked at each

other. What about an ostrich on the loose?

Outside, someone was coming up the path.

Not an ostrich.

It was Luke.

"Hey." He bent to catch his breath. "Something happened at the zoo. Come and see. My dad's the zoo doctor. He'll show us."

They stood up and hurried toward the Baby Zoo.

Luke's dad was waiting. He pointed to a window.

First they saw a nest. It was empty.

"All the ostriches lay their eggs in one nest," Luke's dad said. "But then . . ."

They saw.

A few ostriches were inside. Babies wandered around underneath them.

"They're born with their feathers, ready to go," Luke's dad said. "All the grown-up ostriches watch out for them."

Luke leaned toward the window. "They've been here for days."

Sumiko pulled out her pad. She began to draw.

No ostriches were missing,

Torry thought. Then what was hiding behind the sticker bush?

Sumiko looked at her and nodded.

They both knew . . .

An animal was at large.

Was it scary?

Maybe, Tori thought.

CHAPTER 7

IT wasn't dark yet. And it was still hot.

Could she have dreamed those sounds? She tried not to think of her messed-up nails.

"I guess we could go to the patio and turn on the hose," she told Sumiko.

They sat at the table.

The hose felt cool on their feet.

Tori stood up to fill the feeder.
The seed was almost gone.

"Tough," a voice said.

Had she heard that?

Sumiko turned. "What did you
say?"

Tori shook her head. "I didn't . . ."

Sumiko raised one shoulder.

"Sorry. I thought . . ."

"Tough," the voice said again. Someone began to laugh.

Not a dream. Of course not.

CHAPTER 8

TORI turned off the hose. They hurried inside.

Sumiko tacked her ostrich drawing over the bed.

Tori looked at the bird with its fat feathered body and skinny legs. "Perfect," she said.

Ken was banging something in his room.

OSTRICH

They went down the hall to see.

"What are you doing?" Tori called.

Ken opened the door enough to squeeze through.

"Private." He was laughing. "Important and secret."

He was trying something new again.

If only it worked! "Good luck," Tori told him.

"Thanks," he said.

And then she remembered.

The tiny scraps of paper were still in her pocket.

She and Sumiko went into her bedroom.

She lay the pieces of green paper next to the ones from her pocket.

She moved them up and down.

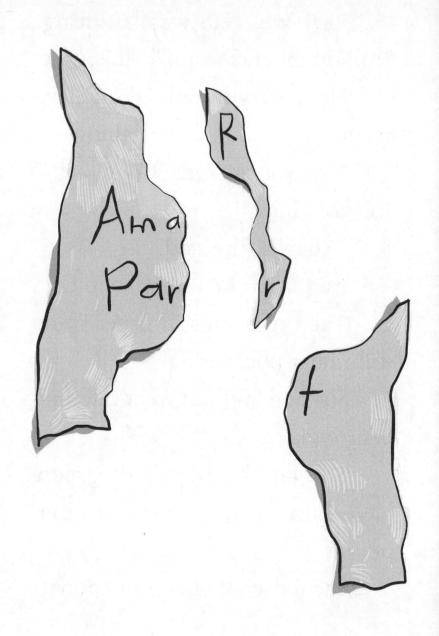

Back and forth.

"Maybe it works like this," she said.

They had to do something.

They had to help.

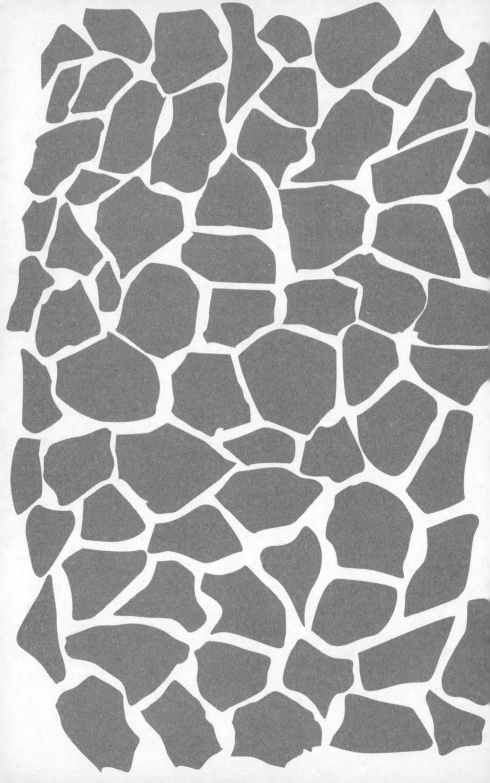

CHAPTER 9

IT was morning. Sumiko was still asleep.

Tori was wide awake.

She looked out at the patio. Two brown sparrows were at the feeder.

A downy woodpecker came next.

Was someone staring at her from the sticker bush?

"Tough," said the voice.

Was that Luke? It sounded like him. A little bit anyway

Tori sank down on the floor. She hid behind the curtain.

She didn't hear the voice again.

Maybe he was gone.

Gone where?

She was going to find out.

She went downstairs and out the front door.

Nana-Next-Door was filling the birdbath. "Everyone needs water on this hot day," she said.

Tori nodded, and kept going. She passed Luke's house.

Luke's little sister, Benita, was playing with a puppy.

"Where's Luke?" Tori asked.

Benita pointed toward the zoo with her thumb. "He's helping my grandfather with the giraffes."

Tori leaned forward. "Does Luke like to scare people?"

Benita leaned forward too. "He scared me once. Whoo!"

"I think he's scaring me too."

Benita frowned. "Maybe not."

Tori shrugged. She marched through the iron zoo gates.

Inside an exhibit, a black leopard lay across a tree branch.

Tori shaded her eyes.

A flamingo strutted by. It must have eaten a pile of shrimp. That's why it looked so pink.

Giraffe Neck was around the corner. Tori looked up at the giraffes.

They were friendly, not like lions or tigers. Especially not like crocodiles.

And there was Luke. He was sweeping the path in front of Giraffe Neck.

Tori ducked behind Lions' Lair.

One of the lions yawned.

It had more teeth than she could count.

She stood on tiptoes to see.

Luke put the broom in the shed. Then he headed down another path.

GIRAFFE NECK

Tori followed him.

He bought a bag of popcorn at the Blue Zoo Stand.

Tori's mouth watered. Too bad her allowance was gone.

She'd spent it on . . .

She couldn't remember.

Luke ran just ahead of her. He looked over his shoulder.

Tori jumped back.

Luke turned the corner. He raced down another path.

He was really fast.

Tori hurried.

Luke stopped at Penguin Place. He looked over his shoulder.

Tori took a breath.

He was coming toward her.

She was ready to run.

Too late.

He was right there.

Staring at her!

CHAPTER 10

"GOTCHA," Luke said.

Tori waved at the popcorn stand. "I was . . ."

"You were following me."

"I guess so." She gulped. "You think I'm tough?"

He blinked. "I don't know. Maybe."

She held out her wrist. "See, I even got a scratch."

"Ouch," he said.

"From the sticker bush. You'd better stop hiding there too."

He shook his head. "I never go near those things."

Could she believe him?

He held out the bag of popcorn. "Want some?"

"Thanks." She took a handful.

"Say *tough*," she said after she swallowed.

"Tough," he said.

Too bad his mouth was filled with popcorn. It didn't sound

like the voice behind the sticker bush. It sounded like crunching popcorn.

She thought of something else. She'd show him what happened to her nails the first time someone was in the bush. "Did you mess up my nails?"

Luke blinked. "What?"

She waved her fingers.

"Polka dots." He looked closer. "Something sharp did that."

He was right.

Luke knew a lot.

Maybe too much.

Luke's dad, the zoo doctor,

popped his head out from the Baby Zoo.

"I need some help, Luke." He smiled at Tori.

Luke held out the popcorn bag again. "See you," he said.

Tori took another handful.

Back home, Sumiko and Ken were eating breakfast. Eggs with cheese.

"The worst," Tori said.

Sumiko grinned. "The best."

Tori grabbed a banana instead. "Let's go out to the patio," she said.

She didn't want to go alone. But she needed cool water from the hose.

"I'll have a surprise soon," Ken said.

What was that about? She raised her shoulders.

Sumiko did too.

CHAPTER 11

SHE and Sumiko sank down on the patio.

Tori took a bite of her banana.

The banana was perfect; so was the water on her feet.

She pulled out the missing papers.

"Hey," Sumiko said. "It's not windy."

"Just hot," Tori said.

"Then why is the butterfly bush moving?"

Tori looked at the kitchen door. It was only a few steps away.

No. She wasn't going to run inside.

Not this time.

She left the banana on the table.

At the edge of the patio, she pulled a branch aside.

"Ouch!"

She stared in.

It was Luke's little sister, Benita.

"Hey!" Tori said.

Benita crawled out. Her arms

were covered with scratches. She had stickers in her hair.

"I want to hear it," Tori said.

"What?" Benita rubbed her arm.

"Say *tough*."

Benita put her hands on her hips. "Luke told me all about it. You think I'm the one now?"

"What's happening?" Sumiko asked.

"I'm hiding in here to help my brother," Benita said. "I'm looking for the bad guy."

Tori took a breath. She had to believe Benita. She would have helped Ken too.

Benita marched off the patio.

There was another sound. Not tough. Almost like a frog. Galumph. Galumph.

A frog?

CHAPTER 12

KEN jumped out from the other side of the patio. "It worked!" he yelled.

He went to the sticker bush. He pulled string after him. Then he took out a cup and wet cloth.

There was a flurry of branches. Tori saw a flash of green.

"My latest experiment from a book," Ken said. "How to sound like a frog."

"Not a missing frog," Sumiko said.

"No." Tori took a bite of banana.

She was thinking, though. She was using her brain.

Something was hiding behind the sticker bush.

It was something that liked the patio. Why?

A gray catbird flew past.

Something that liked the feeder seed?

Something green?

She went inside. She raced into her bedroom and threw herself on the floor.

She sneezed about four times.

Too bad she hadn't dusted the rug better.

Ah, but there they were: pictures of sparrows, of red-winged blackbirds, of . . .

She dashed outside.

She tiptoed across the patio.

"Hey," she whispered. "I solved the mystery."

"Tough," came the voice.

"It's a rare bird," she said. "An Amazon parrot missing from the zoo."

"A talking bird," Sumiko said.

Sumiko sat at the table. She played with the torn papers. "You're right," she said. "It all fits."

"Wow," Ken said. "Hanging out in our sticker bush. Eating the seed. A parrot who says . . ."

"Tough," came the voice.

Tori tiptoed to the sticker bush.

She pulled a branch aside. Never mind the scratch she'd get.

She had to get a look at the bird.

It sat on the highest branch, staring down at her with shiny dark eyes. Its coat was bright green.

It threw its head back and . . . Was it laughing?

Tori smiled as she ran across to Nana-Next-Door's house. Nana would bring the bird back where it would be safe.

And then, Tori would write her life story.

It wouldn't be boring.

She lived on Zoo Lane, next to a zoo.

She had a brother who tried new things. And one of them worked.

Her cousin and best friend came from Tokyo, Japan.

She kept Kimi indoors. It helped the wildlife.

And she had found a rare Amazon parrot. And mostly because of a dusty rug.

Miss Raymond would love it.

She loved it too.

AMAZON PARROTS

Some parrots are green with red tails. Others have bright blue fronts. Some have orange wings, and some have yellow on their foreheads. Parrots are friendly. They can be trained to talk, sounding like people. *Tough!* Some live as long as forty or fifty years.

OSTRICHES

They're the largest birds, and because they can weigh up to three hundred pounds, they can't fly! But they can run! When running long distances, they can travel about thirty miles an hour. But when they're in a hurry, watch out! They can run sixty miles an hour when they are covering short distances. They like veggies, but will settle for insects if they have to.

READ MORE OF THE

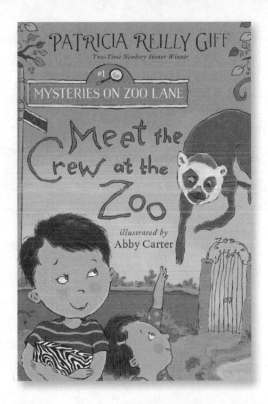

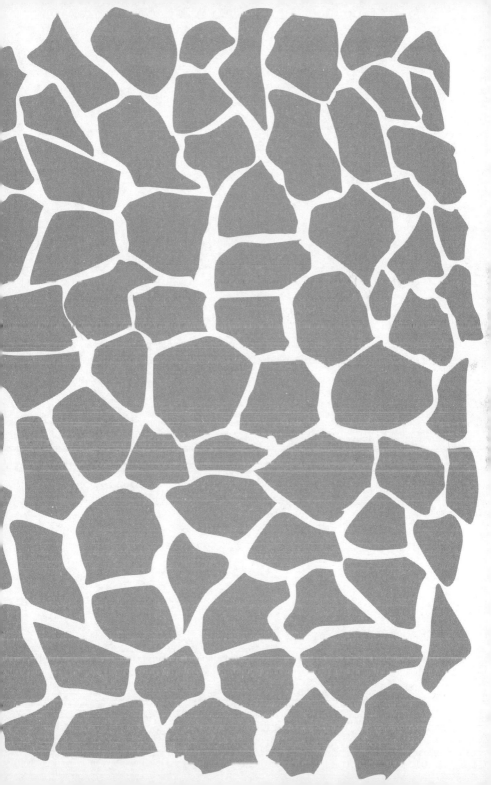